Snuggle Up

Written by Jamie French
Illustrated by Gail Yerrill

IMAGINE THAT

Licensed exclusively to Imagine That Publishing Ltd
Tide Mill Way, Woodbridge, Suffolk, IP12 1AP, UK
www.imaginethat.com
Copyright © 2021 Imagine That Group Ltd
All rights reserved
0 2 4 6 8 9 7 5 3 1
Manufactured in China

Written by Jamie French
Illustrated by Gail Yerrill

ISBN 978-1-80105-193-4

A catalogue record for this book is available from the British Library

Pitter-patter, pitter-patter went the rain.
'Let's find a dry place to snuggle up,'
said the elephants.

'Let's find somewhere cosy,'
said the kangaroos.

'Let's buzz in a huddle,'
said the wasps and the bees.

'Let's scuttle from the raindrops,' said the ants.

'Let's squeeze into the warm!'
said the hippo.

'There's room in here for more!'
called his friends.

'Let's snuggle up ...

... and hug like bears do best!'
said the bears.

'No more rain, thank you!' said the monkeys. 'Can we come in and cuddle up, too?'

'Is there room in there for us?'
snorted the chilly pigs.

'*Snuffle, snuffle!* It's wet out here!'

'Let's shuffle to the shelter,'
said the tortoises, going as
fast as they could.

'Let's follow the crowd and nuzzle nice and close,' said the zebras.

'*Cluck, cluck, cluck!*' went the chickens.

'A comfy coop is what we need!'

Inside, it was snug ... and
cosy ... and toasty-warm ...

Has it stopped raining yet?

'Not yet. Maybe tomorrow,'
said the elephant.
'Snuggle up, everyone.'

Pitter-patter,
pitter-patter
went the rain.